D1543928

To:

From:

To my wife, Jill, an answer to many prayers that I might find true love. —GL

For my mom, whose fierce and unconditional love made me who I am. —CM

For Simon, James and Lucia, who fill my world with love. —LA

Discover other books in the series!

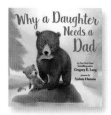 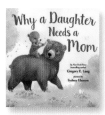  

Why We Need Love © 2004, 2022 by Gregory E. Lang

Text adapted for picture book by Craig Manning

Illustrations by Lisa Alderson

Cover and internal design © 2022 by Sourcebooks

Sourcebooks and the colophon are registered trademarks of Sourcebooks.

The full color art was prepared using mixed media.

Published by Sourcebooks Wonderland, an imprint of Sourcebooks Kids

P.O. Box 4410, Naperville, Illinois 60567–4410

(630) 961-3900

sourcebookskids.com

Cataloging-in-Publication Data is on file with the Library of Congress.

Source of Production: Worzalla, Stevens Point, Wisconsin, United States of America

Date of Production: October 2022

Run Number: 5024694

Printed and bound in the United States of America.

WOZ 10 9 8 7 6 5 4 3 2 1

Why the World Needs Love

by Gregory E. Lang   pictures by Lisa Alderson

Adapted for picture book by Craig Manning

sourcebooks
wonderland

What makes a life full, and happy, and bright?

A feeling that warms you like summer's sunlight?

What makes your heart feel like a bird in mid-flight?

The answer is easy: It's love!

When we hear "I love you," it makes us feel warm,

like we're always protected, and safe from the storm.

Love can take many shapes, sizes, and forms,

but it's always right there by your side.

Just like eating, or drinking, or breathing the air,

we're safe in the comfort our loved ones are there.

Simply having them with us, and knowing they care,

life takes on a happy meaning.

We need love because it makes us know we belong,

like a perfect rhyme in a beautiful song!

Friends and family can help make you feel strong

and give you the courage to grow.

See, you'll go many places over the years.

You'll experience joy and shed a few tears.

You'll celebrate life, with laughter and cheers,

and you couldn't do those things without love.

Because love keeps us going when the days feel tough.

It's the good thing that drives us through all the bad stuff.

No matter how hard things might get, it's always enough

to know there's a hug at home waiting.

Love can tie us together in more ways than one,

like a friend to a friend, or a dad to a son.

Try to cherish those bonds, because in the long run

a life full of love is a gift.

The things you enjoy will always mean more

if you enjoy them with someone you love and adore.

Be it ice cream, or stories, or a dance 'round the floor

the best things in life should be shared.

And speaking of sharing, you'll know that you're blessed

when you're laughing along with those you know best!

Laughter so hard that it hurts your whole chest?

That's love in its purest form.

Someday, you'll grow up and you'll leave your home.

You'll travel to New York, or Sweden, or Rome!

But no matter what you do, or how far you roam,

know that home's always there in your heart.

Because home isn't just a dot on a map,

or a place that you see in your dreams when you nap.

It's a gift deep down that you can always unwrap.

It's the love that you feel every day.

It's the love that you have for your father and mother,

for your grandma and grandpa, or your sister or brother,

for your friends, and your pets, and all of the others

who help you make sense of the world.

So try to remember, day in and day out

that love is the one thing that life's all about.

Whether said in a whisper or screamed in a shout,

"I love you" means more than you know.

Think of it this way: what makes you feel glad?

What cheers you up even when you get sad?

What was there on the best days that you've ever had?

Most times, the answer is love.

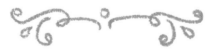

Love is there in the memories you'll always hold dear.

It's there at the holidays, giving us cheer!

It's there in most songs that you'll ever hear.

It's the way that you feel when you smile.

So smile, dear one, because the world needs more love:

More happiness, more laughter, more sunshine above.

Love with all of your heart, for the one thing we're sure of,

is that love is what everyone needs.